Very Short
Fairy Stories
A Treasury

Little, Brown and Company

Hachette Book Group
1290 Avenue of the Americas, New York, NY 10104
Visit us at lb-kids.com

LB kids is an imprint of Little, Brown and Company.
The LB kids name and logo are trademarks of Hachette Book Group, Inc.

The publisher is not responsible for websites (or their content)
that are not owned by the publisher.

First Edition: February 2015

Beck and the Case of the Pesky Hummingbird and *Beck and the Berry Battle* originally published as *Beck and the Great Berry Battle* in 2006 by Disney Publishing Worldwide, an imprint of Disney Book Group. • *Lily's Surprise Seed* and *Lily and the Outstanding Olives* originally published as *Lily's Pesky Plant* in 2006 by Disney Publishing Worldwide, an imprint of Disney Book Group. • *Rani in the Mermaid Lagoon, Rani Saves a Sea Horse,* and *A Tour of Mermaid Lagoon* originally published as *Rani in the Mermaid Lagoon* in 2006 by Disney Publishing Worldwide, an imprint of Disney Book Group. • *The Case of the Curious Cannonball* originally published as *Tinker Bell Takes Charge* in 2006 by Disney Publishing Worldwide, an imprint of Disney Book Group. • *Fira and the Firefly Flu, Fira's Friends,* and *Fira and the Never Mines* originally published as *Fira and the Full Moon* in 2006 by Disney Publishing Worldwide, an imprint of Disney Book Group. • *A Fairy Berry Cake* originally published as *Tinker Bell's Tea Party* in 2008 by Disney Press, an imprint of Disney Book Group. • *The Case of the Fickle Frogs* and *The Thirsty Flowers* originally published as *Tinkering Tink* in 2008 by Disney Press, an imprint of Disney Book Group. • *Hem's Dress Dilemma* originally published as *A Dozen Fairy Dresses* in 2010 by Random House Children's Books, a division of Random House, Inc. • *A Very Fairy Game of Hide-and-Seek* originally published as *A Game of Hide-and-Seek* in 2009 by Random House Children's Books, a division of Random House, Inc. • *Rani's Rainy Day* and *Rani's Swap Meet* originally published as *Rani and the Three Treasures* in 2006 by Disney Press, an imprint of Disney Book Group. • *The Missing Fairy Crown* originally published as *Vidia and the Fairy Crown* in 2006 by Disney Publishing Worldwide, an imprint of Disney Book Group. • *The Boat Race* originally published as *Prilla's Prize* in 2006 by Disney Press, an imprint of Disney Book Group. • *What Do the Fairies Do?* originally published as *Nature's Little Helpers* in 2011 by Random House Children's Books, a division of Random House, Inc. • *The Famous Fairy Race, Part I* and *The Famous Fairy Race, Part II* originally published as *The Great Fairy Race* in 2008 by Random House Children's Books, a division of Random House, Inc. • *A Fairy Berry Bake Off, Part I* and *A Fairy Berry Bake Off, Part II* originally published as *The Fairy Berry Bake-Off* in 2008 by Random House Children's Books, a division of Random House, Inc. • *Bess Paints a Picture* originally published as *Picture Perfect* in 2006 by Disney Press, an imprint of Disney Book Group. • *A Squirrel-y Situation* originally published as *The Pixie Mix-Up* in 2007 by Disney Press, an imprint of Disney Book Group. • *Beck's Missing Bunny* originally published as *Beck's Bunny Secret* in 2010 by Random House Children's Books, a division of Random House, Inc.

Library of Congress Control Number: 2014946476

ISBN 978-0-316-28348-9

10 9 8 7 6 5 4 3 2 1

SC

Printed in China

Very Short Fairy Stories

A Treasury

LITTLE, BROWN & COMPANY
LB kids

Table of Contents

A Very Fairy Guide

The Fairies

Tinker Bell
(nickname: Tink)

Tinker Bell is a pots-and-pans fairy. She loves anything metal that can be cracked or dented, and the toughest repair jobs are her favorite. Tink is impatient, but there is no fairy more loyal and quick to fly to someone's rescue.

Vidia

Vidia is the fastest of the fast-flying fairies. At times, Vidia can be selfish, but she learned the importance of friendship at fairy summer camp and now she gets along with the fairies—most of the time. She lives in the sour-plum tree.

Fawn

Fawn is a lively and mischievous animal-talent fairy. She loves pranks and going on adventures, but most of all, she loves all her furry (and sometimes slimy) friends: skunks, frogs, bunnies, and many more!

Silvermist
(nickname: Sil)

Silvermist is a water-talent fairy. She is known for being kind and generous to her fairy friends.

Rosetta

Rosetta is a charming and beautiful garden-talent fairy. She loves dressing up almost as much as she loves tending her garden.

Iridessa
(nickname: Dessa)

Iridessa is a smart, no-nonsense light-talent fairy. Iridessa likes to be prepared, and she always does things by the book. She is a very loyal friend.

Beck

Beck is a curious and playful animal-talent fairy. She has a gift for talking to all animals and reading their thoughts and feelings. This makes her a great translator between all the species of Pixie Hollow.

Dulcie

Dulcie is the best baking-talent fairy in Pixie Hollow. Her specialties are her delicious poppy-puff rolls and her huckleberry shortcake. Dulcie is very generous, but she can be bossy in the kitchen.

Bess

Bess is an art-talent fairy. She finds inspiration in nature and can usually be found in her studio with paint splattered on her face and clothing. She loves sharing her art with her fairy friends.

Fira
(nickname: Moth)

Fira is a light-talent fairy, and she can brighten the whole Pixie Dust Tree with her glow! She is responsible for training the fireflies that light Pixie Hollow at night.

Lily

Lily is a very gifted garden-talent fairy. She is generous, patient, and the proud keeper of the most beautiful garden in Pixie Hollow. Lily can communicate with plants and sense if they are happy or sad.

Prilla

Prilla is the first and only Mainland-visiting clapping-talent fairy. She is sweet, optimistic, and always eager to try new things.

Terence

Terence is a dust-keeper fairy and sparrow man. His job is to measure and hand out fairy dust, which enables the fairies to fly.

Rani

Rani is a generous and affectionate water-talent fairy. Her talent allows her to do magical things with water: She can shape it into any form and scoop it up with her hands without losing a drop. She is the only fairy without wings.

Queen Clarion
(nickname: Queen Ree)

Queen Clarion is the noble ruler of Pixie Hollow. She is warm, wise, fair, and compassionate—everything you would want in a queen. She commands respect and honesty from all.

Locations

Pixie Dust Tree

Located in the heart of Pixie Hollow, this is where all the fairies (except Vidia) live and work. Fairy workshops are located on the lower floors while the fairy bedrooms are located on the higher levels.

The Tearoom

    The tearoom is the first room off the corridor from the lobby. Decorated with Never grass wallpaper and fresh flowers, this is where the fairies eat every day. It is Queen Clarion's favorite room.

The Kitchen

Through a swinging door off the tearoom is the kitchen, where the baking fairies spend most of their time. The kitchen is always warm from the oven and filled with delicious baking scents.

Lily's Garden

Located two frog's leaps beyond the Pixie Dust Tree is Lily's beautiful garden. Fairies drop by every day to see the wild rosebushes, poppies, clovers, and other flowers. They can also collect herbs for their potions here.

Potion Shop

A fairy can find the potion shop on the third floor of the Pixie Dust Tree. Dark wood shelves line the walls, each filled with carefully labeled potions, medicines, and plant extracts.

Never Mines

The Never mines are a network of underground mines where fairies can dig for Never silver, Never gold, and various gems. The crystal cave is found inside the mines.

Mermaid Lagoon and Castle

This sparkling blue lagoon is where the mermaids live. Deep under the lagoon is the mermaids' sea castle, framed by freshwater pearls. Inside the castle are a treasure room, a shell museum, and the seaweed gardens.

Very Short Fairy Stories

Beck and the Case of the Pesky Hummingbird

Beck loves all animals big and small, furry and tall.

There is nothing she likes more than speaking with the birds, chipmunks, foxes, and moles.

But, on this particular day, one fussy hummingbird is testing Beck's patience—and the patience of the other residents of Pixie Hollow.

Beck rests on a branch for a nap. The
hummingbird flies above her and sings
loudly, making her ears hurt.

The chipmunks settle inside their log for a spring snooze, and the hummingbird darts inside and startles them.

The fairies and animals decide to teach the excited hummingbird some manners.

One fairy teaches the hummingbird
to sing quietly to fairies before bedtime.

A chipmunk explains that the inside
of the log is perfect for sleeping and that
the outside of the log is perfect for flying.

Eventually, the hummingbird learns
his manners and becomes friends with
all the animals of Pixie Hollow.

The
End

Lily's Surprise Seed

Lily has a talent for making flowers grow.

When she finds a mysterious seed in the forest, she plants it right away.

After lots of digging and watering in the sun, Lily needs to rest. Suddenly, a curious bee arrives.

"What are you waiting for?" he asks.

"I just planted a seed," Lily explains. "I am waiting for it to grow."

"Well, that may take a while," the bee responds.

"You're right!" Lily agrees, and with that, she rests against a mushroom and falls asleep.

After her long nap, a fairy comes
over and wakes her up. She tells Lily
that her seed has sprouted!

Lily flies over to her new plant.
"Another olive tree!" she shouts.

"Let's mark it in our garden book."

Lily and her friend sit down and make a note. She is so proud of her garden and can't wait for this new olive tree to grow up.

The End

Rani in the Mermaid Lagoon

 One afternoon, Rani visits Tinker
Bell at her workshop because Rani
is feeling sad. It isn't easy being the only
fairy in Pixie Hollow who doesn't have
wings.

"I don't feel like I belong in Pixie Hollow anymore," she says.

"Where do you think you belong?" Tink asks.

"Perhaps the Mermaid Lagoon. I am more like the mermaids than the fairies," Rani replies.

Tinker Bell doesn't agree, but she wishes Rani a safe trip.

That night, Rani finds a leaf boat and makes her way to the Mermaid Lagoon.

The next morning, Rani arrives at the shore of the Mermaid Lagoon. She spots two mermaids resting on moss-covered rocks.

"Hello, fairy," says a mermaid. "What brings you here?"

"My name is Rani, and I am a water-talent fairy, but I have no wings," Rani explains. "I believe I will fit in more with the mermaids."

The mermaids nod in agreement.

The mermaids bring Rani underwater
and show her different kinds of striped
fish and a shiny blue eel. Everything is
so bright and beautiful!

Rani is impressed by the lagoon, but she misses her friends back in Pixie Hollow. She decides to go home.

The mermaids gather to say good-bye. "We hope to see you again soon!" they shout.

The End

The Case of the Curious Cannonball

CRASH! BOOM!
It is early morning, and a loud bang rings throughout Pixie Hollow. Tinker Bell rushes to the Pixie Dust Tree, where she finds a huge cannonball!

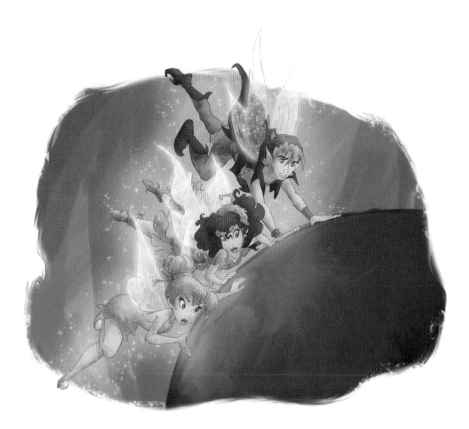

Soon, several fairies arrive to see
the round ball of metal that has landed
smack in the middle of their courtyard.
They work together to try to move it, but
it won't budge!

Tinker Bell must fix this problem. She flies home to brainstorm ideas, and once she has a few, she sets out to clear the courtyard.

First, she asks the brave mice of Pixie Hollow to pull the cannonball away from the Pixie Dust Tree. They try with all their might, but the cannonball only moves a few inches.

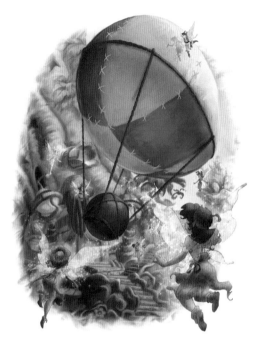

Next, she asks the sewing-talent fairies to make a large air balloon to lift the cannonball up and away.

When a flurry of wind arrives, it raises the cannonball into the sky. The fairies cheer!

But soon after, the cannonball crashes back toward the ground—and fast!

"Oh no," Tink cries. When she moves closer to the cannonball, she realizes it has broken into smaller parts.

"This is going to be much easier to clean up!" Rosetta shouts. And that is exactly what the fairies do.

The End

Rani Saves a
Sea Horse

While visiting the Mermaid Lagoon, Rani explores a dark underwater cave. Inside the cave she finds a collection of sparkling treasures! She sees a mirror, a headband, and shiny seashells.

She swims back toward the surface with her jewels and shells to show them to her fairy friends back in Pixie Hollow.

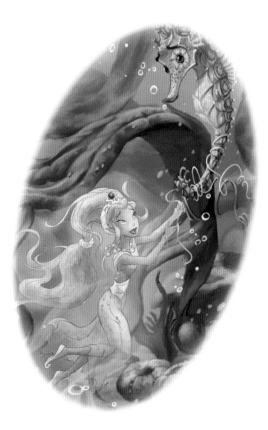

But on her way she encounters a sea horse stuck in some seaweed.

"Oh no! What has happened?" Rani asks aloud. As she gets closer to the sea horse, she notices that his tail is tangled in some string.

She immediately gets to work unraveling the thread and sets the sea horse free!

The sea horse is very thankful to be safe again! He takes his new friend Rani for a ride on his back around the magical Mermaid Lagoon.

The End

Fira and the
Firefly Flu

Fira is a light-talent fairy who takes care of Pixie Hollow's fireflies. The fireflies help provide light at night and work as flashlights when the fairies explore dark tunnels.

One morning, Fira wakes up with a terrible cough and a fever.

"What could have made me sick?" she asks herself.

A garden-talent fairy arrives at her window. She tells Fira that the fireflies have come down with the no-fire flu!

"Oh no!" Fira shouts. "My poor little fireflies." She realizes that the reason she is not feeling well is because her fireflies are ill.

She gets up and asks her friends for help. She must take care of her sick bugs, even if she feels ill herself.

First, she stops by Tinker Bell's home and asks if she can brew her famous flu-fighting tea. Next, she heads to Pixie Hollow's laboratory to pick up healing potions and medicines.

She is in such a hurry that she knocks the medicine off the shelf, but she saves it just in time!

After Fira collects the medicine, she heads to the firefly nursery to help bring the fireflies back to health. She drinks some of the potion, too, and starts to feel better right away.

Fairies from all over Pixie Hollow help to take care of the fireflies. They give them medicine, tea, and potions.

Just like Fira, the fireflies recover quickly and are ready to go back to work.

Fira is happy that all is well with her fireflies and that Pixie Hollow is back to normal again.

The End

Beck and the
Berry Battle

One sunny afternoon, Beck visits a fairy friend for tea and muffins. The friends catch up on all the latest news in Pixie Hollow.

Without warning, the table shakes, and their cups of tea quiver and spill.

"Oh my!" says Beck. "I wonder what that was."

As soon as Beck steps outside, a large purple berry soars past her and smashes into the grass.

"Yikes!" Beck cries. "Where did that berry come from?"

When Beck looks out into the open field, she spots a chipmunk in trouble! Berries are flying at him from every direction.

"Help!" the chipmunk cries.

Beck runs over and hugs the chipmunk close. They hurry across the field and find shelter in a hollow log.

"Just in time," says Beck, watching a berry crash where they were just standing. "What is going on?"

"It's the great berry battle!" the
chipmunk responds enthusiastically.

Beck is confused. "You are throwing
berries at one another for fun?" she asks.

"Yes!" shouts the chipmunk. "It's messy,
but cleanup is always delicious!"

Beck laughs. Even though a berry
battle isn't her cup of tea, she can see that
the chipmunks are having a berry blast.

The
End

Lily and the Outstanding Olives

Lily is planting olive trees all over Pixie Hollow, so she wants to make sure she knows everything there is to know about growing them.

She visits another garden-talent fairy and asks to borrow her gardening book.

"What do you need it for?" the fairy asks.

"I would like to read about olives—how to plant them and how to grow them," replies Lily.

"Oh, me too!" the fairy responds.

The fairies sit in the garden to read the gardening book. Rani, a water-talent fairy, joins them.

"It says here," the garden-talent fairy starts, "that the olive is a species of small tree that is short and squat. The fruit is a small—"

"Fruit?" cries Lily. "I didn't know it was a fruit."

"Yes, a fruit," Rani replies. "And they are harvested in the green and purple stages."

"Fascinating," Lily adds.

The fairies learn so much about the olive trees that they decide to share their findings with the rest of Pixie Hollow.

"It is best for us to know all about the nature that surrounds us," Lily announces. "This way we can take care of our plants and animals properly."

All of Pixie Hollow agrees. The fairies decide to hold a nature class each week from now on.

The
End

A Fairy Berry Cake

Tinker Bell and Rani love to have tea by the pond. They talk about their talents, their friends, and their futures.

"This tea is delicious," Tink says. "But it's also making me very hungry."

"Let's get all the fairies together and bake a cake!" Rani shouts.

"Excellent idea!" cries Tink.

The two fairies hurry to gather all their fairy friends.

They find Beck and Lily near
a honey tree.

"We are going to make a cake to
eat while we drink this delicious tea!"
Rani shouts.

"What a wonderful idea," says Beck.

"I will bring some of this delicious
honey," adds Lily.

Next, the fairies collect blue
huckleberries. Tinker Bell holds
the sack while Lily fills it up!

The fairies bring the ingredients to the kitchen.

After a few hours, Dulcie comes out carrying a beautiful huckleberry shortcake!

"It's wonderful!" Tinker Bell shouts. "I cannot wait to eat a slice."

The fairies set the table with a spiderweb tablecloth, plenty of teacups, leaf saucers, and the mouthwatering cake.

"Fairies," Tink starts, "I want to
thank you for all your help today. Rani
and I couldn't have made such a beautiful
cake without you."

"Cheers!" all the fairies sing.

The
End

The Case of the Fickle Frogs

The fairies are tidying up the Pixie Dust Tree when Tinker Bell hears a cry for help.

"I must go and investigate," Tink tells Lily. Lily nods, watching her fly away.

Tinker Bell arrives at the stream and finds Beck and a cluster of unhappy frogs.

"Tink!" Beck cries. "These Never frogs are being so fickle. Some are thirsty, some are too hot, and the rest want to be fed—all at once!"

Tinker Bell has an idea!

Tinker Bell gets to work right away! She builds a water-sprinkler-feeding-shade machine that will shower water over thirsty frogs, create cool shade for warm frogs, and feed Never fruit seeds to hungry frogs!

Once her machine is finished, she pushes it to the bank of the stream.

"I can't wait to see this machine in action," she says.

Tinker Bell fills the machine with fruit seeds and water.

Soon enough, the thirsty frogs receive water, the warm frogs receive shade, and the hungry frogs receive fruit seeds.

"You're a genius!" Beck cries. "I have never seen the Never frogs happier."

Tinker Bell beams with satisfaction. She loves saving the day!

The
End

Hem's Dress Dilemma

"Attention, fairies," Queen Clarion says. "We are going to hold a ball in honor of Purple Moon Night."

The fairies shout with excitement. They cannot wait to wear beautiful dresses to the ball.

Hem, on the other hand, is nervous. The fairies want her help trimming and sewing their gowns.

Hem hopes she can get her dress plus the fairies' dresses done in time for the ball.

Hem gets to work right away. She cuts, she pins, she tucks, and she sews and sews and sews! She has dozens of flowers, leaves, and buttons to stitch onto the dresses.

"I'll add this purple flower here," she says aloud. "And this green ruffle here. I just need to take in the waist of this pink dress."

Voilà! Hem finishes all the dresses.
She even makes something special
for herself.

When Hem arrives at the ball, she sees all the fairies in their beautiful dresses. It makes her feel proud.

"Your dress is magnificent," Tinker Bell says. "I love the layers of color!"

"Thank you," responds Hem. "I have all of you to thank. You all are an inspiration to my fashion designs!"

The fairies dance the night away in celebration of the Purple Moon.

The
End

A Tour of Mermaid Lagoon

After a few visits to the Mermaid Lagoon, Rani wants to bring her fairy friends and show them how beautiful it is.

She finds one of the mermaids and asks if she can bring Tinker Bell, Vidia, and Lily to visit.

"Of course," the mermaid responds. "But you can only show them the outdoor fountains because unlike you, the other fairies have wings. Winged fairies are not safe in the water."

"Oh, yes!" Rani says. "This is going to be wonderful."

Rani climbs onto Brother Dove and flies back to Pixie Hollow to tell her friends the exciting news. She will finally be able to share the Mermaid Lagoon with them!

She picks up Tinker Bell, Vidia, and Lily, and they fly back to the lagoon. Brother Dove lands in front of the most extravagant fountain.

"Wow," Tinker Bell says. "I can't take my eyes off it."

"Pretty impressive," says Vidia.

"No wonder you come here all the time!" adds Lily.

Rani is happy that her friends love the Mermaid Lagoon.

"Thank you for coming," Rani says.

"It was our pleasure!" the fairies shout.

Tink, Vidia, and Lily fly back before it is too dark, but Rani stays behind. She wants one more look at the underwater castle.

"I really wish my friends could see this, too," Rani says to the mermaids. "This castle would blow them away."

For now, the underwater castle is for her and the mermaids only.

The End

Disney FAIRIES

A Very Fairy Game of Hide-and-Seek

Tinker Bell flies over the garden and notices Pixie Hollow is quiet and still.

Where have all the fairies gone? she wonders. She hears a giggle and flies close to the tulip from which it is coming. Inside she finds Rosetta!

"What are you doing in here?" Tink asks.

"The fairies want to play hide-and-seek!" Rosetta shouts. "Can you find us all?"

Tinker Bell is ready for the challenge. She flies off to find Fira, Bess, Silvermist, Fawn, Iridessa, Nettle, and Rani.

Tinker Bell looks high and low for the fairies.

She looks behind a spiderweb and under a pinecone. She checks every leaf in the garden.

Atop one leaf she finds Fira! "You got me!" Fira cries.

Next, she finds Bess behind a rock. Her blue footprints led Tink right to her hiding spot!

Tinker Bell finds
Silvermist behind a bog
and Fawn in a nest.

She finds Iridessa
hiding with the fireflies.

Nettle is in a cocoon.

Tinker Bell
has one fairy left
to find!

Tinker Bell is puzzled. She wonders if there is anywhere in Pixie Hollow she hasn't looked.

"I know!" she shouts. "The Mermaid Lagoon."

She flies to the lagoon to investigate, but she only finds mermaids and a large rock. She takes a quick peek behind the rock… and finds Rani! She is playing with a ball of water.

Tinker Bell is beaming. She loves playing hide-and-seek with her friends, but she loves it more when they are all back together!

The End

Rani's Rainy Day

Rani wakes up happy and full of
energy. The sun is shining, the sky
is blue, and a perfect breeze is blowing
through Pixie Hollow.

Rani finds her best friend, Prilla. They go for a walk and then rest on mushrooms in the field.

Suddenly, the two fairies feel a raindrop splash between them.

"Oh no!" cries Rani. "I was looking forward to a day with no rain."

"But you are a water-talent fairy," Prilla responds. "You love the rain."

"I do," Rani says. "But I also enjoy relaxing in the sunshine."

The rain continues to fall, coming down harder and harder.

"Let's make the best of this rainy day!" Prilla shouts. "I want to splash in the lake with you."

Rani agrees and uses her water
talent to create fountains on which
the two fairies can perch. They splash,
squirt, and spray water everywhere!

Prilla gets out and ribbons of water dance around her. "This is incredible!" she shouts.

Bess and Tinker Bell join the fairies to play with all the water, too.

"Look what I made!" shouts Bess. "A water mirror."

Tinker Bell steps in front and sees her reflection. She smiles.

That evening, Rani sits down with Brother Dove and tells him about her rainy day.

"I was looking forward to a day of sunshine," she explains. "But I am happy the rain came because it made all the fairies happy. And that makes me happy."

The End

The Missing
Fairy Crown

Queen Clarion asks the fairies to gather in the Fairy-Tale Theater because she has an announcement to make.

"Fairies," she says, "my crown is missing! I need two volunteers to help me find it. The reward is an endless supply of cupcakes."

Prilla's hand shoots up immediately.

"Thank you, Prilla," the queen says.
"Now Prilla will choose the second
participant."

"I choose...Vidia!" Prilla shouts. Vidia
is not happy with Prilla's choice.

The two fairies search high and low around Pixie Hollow. They check the kitchen, the laundry room, the fairies' bedrooms, and the crystal cave.

"We're never going to find this crown," Vidia growls. "Just look how many objects are at the bottom of this cave."

Suddenly, the fairies slip on some buttons and tumble down a narrow tunnel. The tunnel lets out into a room filled with hundreds of crowns!

"Lucky us!" Prilla shouts. "It looks like we have a good chance of finding Queen Clarion's crown down here."

"There are hundreds, if not thousands, of crowns down here, Prilla," says Vidia. "This is going to take forever!"

Vidia falls backward onto the mound of crowns. When she lands, a crown goes flying in the air and lands on her head.

"Vidia! You found it!" Prilla exclaims. The two fairies laugh.

As soon as they arrive back in Pixie Hollow, Vidia delivers Queen Clarion her crown.

"I am so proud of you both," Queen Clarion says. "You have returned my crown, which means it is time for your reward."

Vidia and the queen look over at a table of sweet treats to find Prilla already helping herself to a cupcake. They smile at each other and join her to celebrate their success.

The End

Fira's Friends

Fira is very excited because three brand-new light-talent fairies will be visiting Pixie Hollow!

She gobbles her breakfast and talks about her plans to show the fairies around Pixie Hollow. She wants to bring them to the Pixie Dust Tree, the Never mines, and their special guest bedroom!

At noon, the three light-talent fairies arrive in Pixie Hollow. Their names are Sparkle, Helios, and Glory. Fira and some other curious garden-talent and light-talent fairies welcome them.

Fira leads the trio around Pixie
Hollow. She cannot wait to show them
all her favorite places.

First, she brings the three fairies to Lily's garden.

Sparkle, Helios, and Glory are impressed with Lily's flowers.

"This is such a beautiful blue flower," says Sparkle.

"It is the most special flower in my garden," Lily responds. "Please don't get too close. My flowers are very sensitive!"

Sparkle backs away slowly, still admiring the pretty bloom.

"Let's keep moving," Fira says. "We have so much more to see!"

Next, Fira brings the fairies to the potion workshop inside the Pixie Dust Tree.

The young fairies gaze around the room at the shelves filled with potions, medicines, and plant extracts. Glory reaches to grab a jar off the shelf.

"Stop!" Fira shouts. "We need to be very careful. Please do not touch anything."

"Okay," Glory agrees. She spins around and clumsily knocks a jug off the shelf, spilling its contents onto a cactus.

Suddenly, the cactus grows three
times in size!

"We have to get out of here!"
cries Fira.

Fira decides it's time to bring the fairies to their special bedroom. Sparkle, Helios, and Glory are tired after exploring.

"Wow," Glory says when they reach the golden doors. "This room is stunning."

"Good night," says Fira. "I hope you enjoyed Pixie Hollow today."

"We did!" the three fairies answer in unison.

With that, Fira goes to bed.

The
End

Fira and the
Never Mines

During a full moon, the mining fairies must work hard because the Never mines fill up with colorful gems, stunning silver, and gleaming gold.

The fairies collect the stones and metals to decorate Pixie Hollow.

The mining fairies use special tools that help them whittle the walls of the Never mines.

Fira, a light-talent fairy, volunteers to help the mining fairies.

Inside the Never caves, it is very dark, so Fira uses her light talent to brighten the path to the gems and metals.

Cheese the mouse also volunteers to carry heavy rocks.

The mining fairies get to work right away! CLINK! CLINK!

Fira flies to the top of the cave and starts choosing the precious stones one by one. She takes several trips, but she gets every last stone!

"Thank you!" shout the mining fairies. "We could not have finished without you and Cheese."

The fairies give Fira a red gem and a pink gem to decorate her own room.

The
End

The Boat Race

Prilla is taking her afternoon walk around her favorite stream when suddenly Rani and some water-talent fairies approach her.

"Come join the Leaf-Boat Race," Rani says.

Prilla looks at the leaf boats floating in
a perfect line at the edge of the water.

"I have never been in a boat race
before," Prilla admits. "But I would love
to join in!"

"First, you must choose a leaf boat," Rani says.

Prilla points to a modest purple boat. It is small and slender, which she believes will make her fast in the water.

"Great choice," Rani says. "Hop in!"

Just as Prilla settles into her leaf boat, the bell rings to signal the start of the race!

Prilla dips her paddle in the water, but her boat glides the wrong way! She pulls in the opposite direction, and her boat tips from side to side.

"Pull the paddle from front to back, not side to side," Rani shouts.

Prilla plunges the paddle and follows Rani's directions, but she makes the boat tip, and she falls overboard!

"Oh no!" Prilla cries. "I definitely won't be winning this race."

Prilla swims to the lakeshore and begins to cry.

"Prilla, what's wrong?" Tink asks.

"I just wish I had finished the race," she whimpers. "I am no good at leaf-boat racing!"

"It was your first try," Rani says. "With practice, you will get better. Now, we have something special for you."

"I present this ribbon to you," Tinker Bell announces, "for trying a new sport and giving it all you've got!"

Prilla blushes with pride. She feels like a winner after all.

The End

What Do the Fairies Do?

The fairies have many different talents that help bring the seasons to Pixie Hollow.

They make icicles glitter in winter, flowers bloom in spring, encourage birds to sing in summer, and change the colors of the leaves in fall.

The fairies also work together to take care of the animals in Pixie Hollow.

Fawn, an animal-talent fairy, talks to the animals to find out exactly where they want to be scratched.

Tinker Bell helps feed carrots to a baby bunny.

Silvermist, a water-talent fairy, collects water drops to give to the baby bunny after her meal.

Fawn also helps take care of a hedgehog and other animals that hibernate in winter.

This hedgehog is having trouble getting to sleep, so Fawn gives him a handmade dandelion-fluff pillow.

"Sleep tight," she whispers.

Silvermist knows how important
water is all year long. She collects
dewdrops with the other water-talent
fairies to use for washing, cooking, and
drinking throughout the year.

Iridessa, a light-talent fairy, catches sunbeams during the day and then gives the light to the fireflies. The glowing bugs help light up Pixie Hollow at night—no electricity required!

Vidia, the fastest fast-flying fairy,
helps the fairies on hot summer days. She
swoops and soars to create cool breezes in
Pixie Hollow.

The fairies are happy for the cooldown.

Rosetta, a garden-talent fairy, is great
at recycling and reusing materials from
her garden. She makes handmade dresses
from petals, leaves, and moss.

The baking-talent fairies are always hard at work. There isn't a fairy in Pixie Hollow who doesn't love to eat, especially strawberry shortcake and blackberry muffins!

The fairies serve food in recycled acorn caps and tea out of baby pumpkins. It's quite a delight!

Working together, there
is nothing the fairies cannot
do! They are nature's little
helpers, and they bring Pixie
Hollow to life with their
special talents.

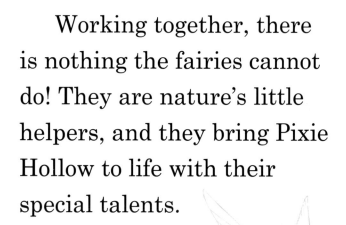

The
End

The Thirsty Flowers

Early one morning in Pixie Hollow, Lily, a garden-talent fairy, flies over to Tink and Beck.

"Can one of you help me with my garden?" she asks. "I need someone to water the plants while I am gone."

"Sure! I can help," Tink responds.

Lily shows Tinker Bell where to find the watering can and how much to sprinkle on each flower.

"That is all there is to it," Lily says. "Pretty easy, right?"

Tinker Bell agrees, but once she starts watering, she realizes it is going to take forever. There are rows and rows of flowers.

Suddenly, Tink has a great idea! She is a tinker fairy after all.

She builds a sprinkler machine that will do the work for her! She uses a long vine to string the watering cans above the flowers, ties one end to a stalk, and holds on to the other end. Then she flies in circles.

Tinker Bell is done watering in no
time! The garden looks beautiful, and
she cannot wait to show Lily.

The
End

The Famous Fairy Race
Part I

Every year in Pixie Hollow, the famous fairy race is held. All the fairies line up at the Pixie Dust Tree and wait for Queen Clarion to start the race.

"On your mark. Get set. Go!" the queen shouts!

Fawn rides a frog. Rani flies on Brother Dove, and Beck rides a squirrel.

Fira flies in a balloon while Silvermist surfs on a wave.

Tinker Bell
rides on a machine
she built.

Lily rides a large
snail, and Bess races
in a wagon pulled by
Cheese the mouse.

The fairies go through many obstacles along the race. They cross a river, pass a tree, and go over a field of grass.

The race is very close, and the fairies
are wing to wing. Who is going to win?

The
End

The Famous Fairy Race
Part II

Suddenly, an accident occurs! Tinker Bell's machine runs over the tail of Beck's squirrel. The two fairies crash. Tink and Beck are out of the race.

Then, Fawn and her frog bump into
Rani and Brother Dove. Brother Dove hits
Fira's balloon, and the balloon sinks.

Fawn, Rani, and Fira's crash causes
Bess and Silvermist to crash, too. What a
mess!

The fairies look up to see Lily
and her snail inching by slowly…
very slowly. They pass the fairies,
and Lily gives a wave.

Bit by bit, Lily and her snail cross the
finish line and win the race!

Queen Clarion meets Lily and declares her the winner of the fairy race. The other fairies join in to congratulate Lily.

In this fairy race, the slow snail is the fastest animal in Pixie Hollow.

The End

Rani's Swap Meet

It is springtime in Pixie Hollow, and the fairies must start their seasonal cleanup.

Rani decides that she will hold a fairy swap meet to get the fairies excited!

Each fairy brings three to four objects they would like to get rid of, but they can swap for other fairies' items, too. Anything not swapped will be recycled.

Rani heads over to the mining fairies' table full of gems and jewels. She finds a special shiny rock that she wants to give to a mermaid at the lagoon.

"She will love it." Rani beams. "She will use it to decorate the underwater castle."

The mining fairies are happy to see their items go to a special home.

The fairies have a wonderful time swapping items. Some fairies swap for dresses; others swap for food, pots and pans, perfume, and much more!

Fira comes over to Rani before the end of the day. "The fairies want you to have this special stone as a thank-you for this wonderful occasion."

Rani smiles. She is proud the swap meet is a success.

The
End

A Fairy Berry Bake Off
Part I

After a long day of playing with fireflies, helping lost animals, and fixing broken pans, the fairies are tired and hungry.

They head to the tearoom to get something to eat.

"I wonder what the baking fairies are baking today," Lily says.

Inside the kitchen, Dulcie is stirring berries over the stove for a delicious tart.

Ginger flies over to investigate. "I am making a tart this afternoon, too," she says.

"Wonderful," Dulcie responds. "The more tarts the better!"

"We cannot bake the same treat," Ginger says. "Unless..."

"We have a fairy berry bake off!" Dulcie shouts.

Ginger agrees, and the fairies start baking right away.

Now they need to make more than just tarts!

They get started on two chocolate cakes. Then they will bake cupcakes, muffins, and more! Who will win the bake off?

The End

A Fairy Berry Bake Off
Part II

The first desserts out are blueberry custard and blackberry cupcakes.

Tinker Bell flies up to Dulcie to grab a cupcake. She cannot wait to eat these sweet treats!

As soon as she eats her cupcake, Ginger
is there with a honey bun. Then, Dulcie
interrupts and asks Tink to try one of her
chocolate-chip muffins.

"There are so many sweets!" Tink
exclaims. "Let me go get the other fairies."

The fairies enter the tearoom again to find cakes filling the tables.

"Dig in," Tink says with a bite of cupcake in her mouth. "Let the fairy berry bake off begin!"

"Don't mind if I do," says Beck.

All the fairies fill their plates and begin eating the delicious treats, but they cannot decide on a winner!

Just as the fairies are about to tell Dulcie and Ginger that they are both winners, the two baking fairies come through the kitchen with a huge cake.

"We decided that we don't want to compete—we want to work together!" Dulcie says. "So we baked this cake for all of you!"

Every fairy is happy and full, but there is always room for one more slice of cake.

The
End

Bess Paints a Picture

It is a sunny afternoon, and Bess arrives at her studio ready to paint! She sings in excitement at the thought of creating a new masterpiece.

She has flown all over Pixie Hollow, gathering inspiration from the nature around her: the animals, the trees, the sky, and the flowers.

243

Bess sits down in front of the white canvas and is about to make her first stroke, but suddenly she cannot think of anything to paint.

"This is odd," Bess says. "I usually have so many ideas after a fly around Pixie Hollow. My mind feels totally blank!"

"Should I paint a chipmunk?" she asks herself. "Or a tree? Maybe I should paint a sunset. Or I can paint a flower. A bluebird? How about if I paint upside down?"

Then, she has it! She moves to the back wall of her studio...

...and creates a beautiful portrait of her five fairy friends!

When the masterpiece is complete, she invites the fairies over to see the painting inspired by them.

"It's wonderful!" they cry. Every fairy is happy.

Bess grins. "Thank you all for being my true inspirations. I could not ask for better fairy friends!"

The End

A Squirrel-y Situation

Rani, a water-talent fairy, is washing the courtyard on a sunny afternoon when she runs out of soap!

Luckily, Lily is close by. Rani asks her to keep an eye on things while she picks up more cleaner.

"I am just running to the kitchen," Rani says. "I will be right back!"

The quickest way to the kitchen is
through the rear entrance of the Pixie
Dust Tree. Rani hurries down the hall, but
as she approaches the tearoom, she hears
a strange noise.

"Chee-chee!"

Rani sees Beck dusting the tearoom
with the help of her squirrel friends.

"Rani!" Beck cries. "I need to gather
nuts for the squirrels. Can you please
watch them while I run out? I just need
you to point out the dusty spots."

"Okay," Rani says. "Sounds easy
enough!"

Rani starts pointing out the dusty spots around the tearoom, but the squirrels are not listening.

Rani sighs. "At this rate, we will never finish dusting before Beck gets back with your treats," she says. "Maybe I can imitate Beck: *Chi-chi!*"

The squirrels freeze.

"They understand!" shouts Rani.

But things suddenly take a turn for the worse. The squirrels run this way and that, knocking over all the tables and chairs.

At this moment, Beck flies in. "What is going on?" she cries.

"I was telling them to dust over there," Rani says. "Like this: *Chi-chi!*"

"Oh no." Beck groans. "That doesn't mean 'dust over there'! It means 'look out for that hawk'!"

The squirrels fly out of the tearoom and wreck everything in their path.

Luckily, Rani and Beck have the best fairy friends.

Tinker Bell, Lily, and a few nearby baking-talent fairies help clean up. They plant new flowers, mop the courtyard, and pick up the tattered tablecloths.

In no time, Pixie Hollow is shimmering and shining again.

The
End

Beck's Missing Bunny

Beck and Fawn are taking care of a baby bunny named Bitty. He was separated from his family and lives in a patch of grass in the meadow.

They go to feed him, but to their surprise, Bitty is missing!

"Oh no!" Beck cries. "I need to start looking everywhere! Bitty is my baby. I can't stand to think he is lost somewhere in Pixie Hollow."

Beck flies off!
She looks for Bitty
everywhere.
First, she checks
the vegetable garden.
She looks behind some
lettuce, underneath a
carrot, and between the green beans.

She looks through all the peas and
then the row of beets. Not even one baby
bunny nibble is found.

Beck gets nervous.
She needs to find Bitty!
She stops by Brother
Dove's nest.
No Bitty.

She searches Tinker
Bell's workshop.
No Bitty.

She looks through
Bess's art studio.
No Bitty.

She explores high
and low in Lily's garden.
No Bitty.

Beck is heartbroken. She flies back to the meadow to check one last time for Bitty.

As she glides over a clover patch, she hears giggling. She decides to take a look.

Bitty and Fawn are inside the cluster of clover!

Instantly, Beck is relieved. "I thought I was never going to find him," she says.

"I found him here munching on these lucky clovers," Fawn says. "I knew you would find us."

The fairies link hands over Bitty. Everyone is happy to be back together again.

The End

Read these other
Disney Fairies storybooks!

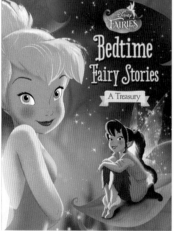

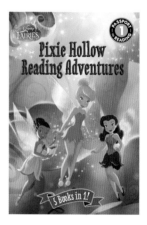